'Into two I'll slice
the hair-seat
of Helga's
kiss-gulper . . .'

The Saga of Gunnlaug Serpent-tongue was written down in Iceland around 1270–1300, although it would have circulated much earlier in oral form. The action is set 990–1010. This translation is taken from *Sagas of Warrior-Poets*, published in Penguin Classics in 2002.

The Saga of Gunnlaug Serpent-tongue

Translated by
Katrina C. Attwood

PENGUIN BOOKS

PENGUIN CLASSICS

UK | USA | Canada | Ireland | Australia
India | New Zealand | South Africa

Penguin Books is part of the Penguin Random House group of companies
whose addresses can be found at global.penguinrandomhouse.com.

This edition published in Penguin Classics 2015
003

Translation copyright © Leifur Eiríksson Publishing Ltd, 1997

The moral right of the translator has been asserted

Set in 9/12.4 pt Baskerville 10 Pro
Typeset by Jouve (UK), Milton Keynes
Printed in Great Britain by Clays Ltd, St Ives plc

A CIP catalogue record for this book is available from the British Library

ISBN: 978-0-141-39786-3

www.greenpenguin.co.uk

This is the saga of Hrafn and of Gunnlaug Serpent-tongue, as told by the priest Ari Thorgilsson the Learned, who was the most knowledgeable of stories of the settlement and other ancient lore of anyone who has lived in Iceland.

1   There was a man named Thorstein. He was the son of Egil, the son of Skallagrim, the son of the hersir Kveldulf from Norway. Thorstein's mother was named Asgerd. She was Bjorn's daughter. Thorstein lived at Borg in Borgarfjord. He was rich and a powerful chieftain, wise, tolerant and just in all things. He was no great prodigy of either size or strength, as his father, Egil, had been. Learned men say that Egil was the greatest champion and duellist Iceland has ever known and the most promising of all the farmers' sons, as well as a great scholar and the wisest of men. Thorstein, too, was a great man and was popular with everyone. He was a handsome man with white-blond hair and fine, piercing eyes.

Scholars say that the Myrar folk – the family descended from Egil – were rather a mixed lot. Some of them were exceptionally good-looking men, whereas others are said to have been very ugly. Many members of the family, such as Kjartan Olafsson, Killer-Bardi and Skuli Thorsteinsson were particularly talented in various ways. Some of them were also great poets, like Bjorn, the Champion of the Hitardal people, the priest Einar Skulason, Snorri Sturluson and many others.

Thorstein married Jofrid, the daughter of Gunnar Hlifarson. Gunnar was the best fighter and athlete among the farmers in Iceland at that time. The second best was Gunnar of Hlidarendi, and Steinthor from Eyri was the third. Jofrid was eighteen years old when Thorstein married her. She was a widow, having previously been married to Thorodd, the son of Tunga-Odd. It was their daughter, Hungerd, who was being brought up at Borg by Thorstein. Jofrid was an independent woman. She and Thorstein had several children, although only a few of them appear in this saga. Their eldest son was named Skuli, the next Kollsvein and the third Egil.

2 It is said that, one summer, a ship came ashore in the Gufua estuary. The skipper was a Norwegian named Bergfinn, who was rich and getting on in years. He was a wise man. Farmer Thorstein rode down to the ship. He usually had the greatest say in fixing the prices at the market, and that was the case this time. The Norwegians found themselves lodgings, and Thorstein himself took the skipper in, since Bergfinn asked him if he could stay at his house. Bergfinn was rather withdrawn all winter, but Thorstein was very hospitable to him. The Norwegian was very interested in dreams.

One spring day, Thorstein asked Bergfinn if he wanted to ride with him up to Valfell. The Borgarfjord people held their local assembly there in those days, and Thorstein had been told that the walls of his booth had fallen in. The Norwegian replied that he would indeed like to go, and they set out later that day, taking a servant of Thorstein's with them. They rode until they arrived at Grenjar farm, which was near Valfell. A poor man named Atli, a tenant of Thorstein's, lived there. Thorstein asked him to come and help them with their work, and to bring with him a turf-cutting spade and a shovel. He did so, and when they arrived at the place where the booths were they all set to work digging out the walls.

It was a hot, sunny day, and when they had finished digging out the walls, Thorstein and the Norwegian sat down inside the booth. Thorstein dozed off, but his sleep was rather fitful. The Norwegian was sitting beside him and let him finish his dream undisturbed. When Thorstein woke up, he was in considerable distress. The Norwegian asked him what he had been dreaming about, since he slept so badly.

'Dreams don't mean anything,' Thorstein answered.

Now when they were riding home that evening, the Norwegian again asked what Thorstein had been dreaming about.

'If I tell you the dream,' Thorstein replied, 'you must explain it as it really is.' The Norwegian said that he would take that risk.

Then Thorstein said, 'I seemed to be back home at Borg, standing outside the main doorway, and I looked up at the buildings, and saw a fine, beautiful swan up on the roof-ridge. I thought that I owned her, and I was very pleased with her. Then I saw a huge eagle fly down from the

3

mountains. He flew towards Borg and perched next to the swan and chattered to her happily. She seemed to be well pleased with that. Then I noticed that the eagle had black eyes and claws of iron; he looked like a gallant fellow.

'Next, I saw another bird fly from the south. He flew here to Borg, settled on the house next to the swan and tried to court her. It was a huge eagle too. As soon as the second eagle arrived, the first one seemed to become rather ruffled, and they fought fiercely for a long time, and I saw that they were both bleeding. The fight ended with each of them falling off the roof-ridge, one on each side. They were both dead. The swan remained sitting there, grief-stricken and dejected.

'And then I saw another bird fly from the west. It was a hawk. It perched next to the swan and was gentle with her, and later they flew off in the same direction. Then I woke up. Now this dream is nothing much,' he concluded, 'and must be to do with the winds, which will meet in the sky, blowing from the directions that the birds appeared to be flying from.'

'I don't think that's what it's about,' said the Norwegian.

'Interpret the dream as seems most likely to you,' Thorstein told him, 'and let me hear that.'

'These birds must be the fetches of important people,' said the Norwegian. 'Now, your wife is pregnant and will give birth to a pretty baby girl, and you will love her dearly. Noble men will come from the directions that the eagles in your dream seemed to fly from, and will ask for your daughter's hand. They will love her more strongly than is reasonable and will fight over her, and both of them will die as a result. And then a third man, coming from the direction from which the hawk flew, will ask for her hand, and she will marry him. Now I have interpreted your dream for you. I think things will turn out like that.'

'Your explanation is wicked and unfriendly,' Thorstein replied. 'You can't possibly know how to interpret dreams.'

'You'll see how it turns out,' the Norwegian retorted.

After this, Thorstein began to dislike the Norwegian, who went away that summer. He is now out of the saga.

3   Later in the summer, Thorstein got ready to go to the Althing. Before he left, he said to his wife, Jofrid, 'As matters stand, you are soon going to have a baby. Now if you have a girl, it must be left out to die, but if it is a boy, it will be brought up.'

When the country was completely heathen, it was something of a custom for poor men with many dependants in their families to have their children exposed. Even so, it was always considered a bad thing to do.

When Thorstein had said this, Jofrid replied, 'It is most unworthy for a man of your calibre to talk like that, and it cannot seem right to you to have such a thing done.'

'You know what my temper is like,' Thorstein replied. 'It will not do for anyone to go against my command.'

Then he rode off to the Althing, and Jofrid gave birth to an extremely pretty baby girl. The women wanted to take the child to Jofrid, but she said that there was little point in that, and had her shepherd, whose name was Thorvard, brought to her.

'You are to take my horse and saddle it,' Jofrid told him, 'and take this child west to Egil's daughter Thorgerd at Hjardarholt. Ask her to bring the child up in secret, so that Thorstein never finds out about it. For I look upon the child with such love that I really have no heart to have it left out to die. Now, here are three marks of silver which you are to keep as your reward. Thorgerd will procure a passage abroad for you out there in the west, and will give you whatever you need for your voyage overseas.'

Thorvard did as she said. He rode west to Hjardarholt with the child and gave it to Thorgerd. She had it brought up by some of her tenants who lived at Leysingjastadir on Hvamms-fjord. She also secured a passage for Thorvard on a ship berthed at Skeljavik in Steingrimsfjord in the north, and made provision for his voyage. Thorvard sailed abroad from there, and is now out of this saga.

Now when Thorstein came back from the Althing, Jofrid told him that the child had been exposed – just as he said it should be – and that the shepherd had run away, taking her horse with him. Thorstein said she had done well, and found himself another shepherd.

Six years passed without this coming out. Then one day Thorstein rode west to Hjardarholt, to a feast given by his brother-in-law Olaf Peacock, who was then the most respected of all the chieftains in the west country. Thorstein was warmly welcomed at Hjardarholt, as might be expected.

Now it is said that, one day during the feast, Thorgerd was

sitting in the high seat talking to her brother Thorstein, while Olaf was making conversation with other men. Three girls were sitting on the bench opposite them.

Then Thorgerd said, 'Brother, how do you like the look of those girls sitting opposite us?'

'Very well,' he replied, 'though one of them is by far the prettiest, and she has Olaf's good looks, as well as the fair complexion and features we men of Myrar have.'

'You are certainly right, brother, when you say that she has the complexion and features of the Myrar men,' Thorgerd said, 'but she has none of Olaf Peacock's looks, since she is not his daughter.'

'How can that be,' Thorstein asked, 'since she's your daughter?'

'Kinsman,' she answered, 'to tell you the truth, this beautiful girl is your daughter, not mine.' Then she told him everything that had happened, and begged him to forgive both her and his wife for this wrong.

'I cannot blame you for this,' Thorstein said. 'In most cases, what will be will be, and you two have smoothed over my own stupidity well enough. I'm so pleased with this girl that I count myself very lucky to have such a beautiful child. But what's her name?'

'She's named Helga,' Thorgerd replied.

'Helga the Fair,' mused Thorstein. 'Now you must get her ready to come home with me.'

And so she did. When he left, Thorstein was given splendid gifts, and Helga rode home to Borg with him and was brought up there, loved and cherished by her father and mother and all her relatives.

4 In those days, Illugi the Black, the son of Hallkel Hrosskelsson, lived at Gilsbakki in Hvitarsida. Illugi's mother was Thurid Dylla, the daughter of Gunnlaug Serpent-tongue. Illugi was the second greatest chieftain in Borgarfjord, after Thorstein Egilsson. He was a great landowner, very strong-willed, and he stood by his friends. He was married to Ingibjorg, the daughter of Asbjorn Hardarson from Ornolfsdal. Ingibjorg's mother was Thorgerd, the daughter of Skeggi from Midfjord. Ingibjorg and Illugi had many children, but only a few of them appear in this saga. One of their sons was named Hermund and another Gunnlaug. They were both promising fellows, and were then in their prime.

It is said that Gunnlaug was somewhat precocious, big and strong, with light chestnut hair, which suited him, dark eyes and a rather ugly nose. He had a pleasant face, a slender waist and broad shoulders. He was very manly, an impetuous fellow by nature, ambitious even in his youth, stubborn in all situations and ruthless. He was a gifted poet, albeit a somewhat abusive one, and was also called Gunnlaug Serpent-tongue. Hermund was the more popular of the two brothers and had the stamp of a chieftain about him.

When Gunnlaug was twelve years old, he asked his father for some wares to cover his travelling expenses, saying that he wanted to go abroad and see how other people lived. Illugi was reluctant to agree to this. He said that people in other countries would not think highly of Gunnlaug when he himself found that he could scarcely manage him as he would wish to at home.

Soon after this, Illugi went out early one morning and saw

that his outhouse was open and that half a dozen sacks of wares had been laid out in the yard, with some saddle-pads. He was very surprised at this. Then someone came along leading four horses; it was his son Gunnlaug.

'I put the sacks there,' he said. Illugi asked why he had done so. He said they would do to help cover his travelling expenses.

'You will not undermine my authority,' said Illugi, 'nor are you going anywhere until I see fit.' And he dragged the sacks back inside.

Then Gunnlaug rode off and arrived down at Borg that evening. Farmer Thorstein invited him to stay and he accepted. Gunnlaug told Thorstein what had happened between him and his father. Thorstein said he could stay as long as he liked, and he was there for a year. He studied law with Thorstein and everyone there thought well of him.

Gunnlaug and Helga often amused themselves by playing board games with each other. They quickly took a liking to each other, as events later bore out. They were pretty much the same age. Helga was so beautiful that learned men say that she was the most beautiful woman there has ever been in Iceland. She had such long hair that it could cover her completely, and it was radiant as beaten gold. It was thought that there was no equal to Helga the Fair throughout Borgarfjord or in places further afield.

Now one day, when people were sitting around in the main room at Borg, Gunnlaug said to Thorstein, 'There is still one point of law that you haven't taught me – how to betroth myself to a woman.'

'That's a small matter,' Thorstein replied, and he taught Gunnlaug the procedure.

Then Gunnlaug said, 'Now you should check whether I've understood properly. I'll take you by the hand and act as though I'm betrothing myself to your daughter Helga.'

'I don't see any need for that,' Thorstein said.

Then Gunnlaug grabbed his hand. 'Do this for me,' he said.

'Do what you like,' Thorstein said, 'but let those present here know that it will be as if this had not been said, and there must be no hidden meaning to it.'

Then Gunnlaug named his witnesses and betrothed himself to Helga. Afterwards, he asked whether that would do. Thorstein said that it would, and everyone there thought it was great fun.

5   There was a man named Onund who lived to the south at Mosfell. He was a very wealthy man, and held the godord for the headlands to the south. He was married, and his wife was named Geirny. She was the daughter of Gnup, the son of Molda-Gnup who settled at Grindavik in the south. Their sons were Hrafn, Thorarin and Eindridi. They were all promising men, but Hrafn was the most accomplished of them in everything. He was a big, strong man, well worth looking at, and a good poet. When he was more or less grown up, he travelled about from country to country and was well respected wherever he went.

Thorodd Eyvindarson the Wise and his son Skafti lived at Hjalli in Olfus in those days. Skafti was Lawspeaker in Iceland at that time. His mother was Rannveig, the daughter of Gnup Molda-Gnupsson, and so Skafti and the sons of Onund were cousins. There was great friendship between them, as well as this blood tie.

Thorfinn Seal-Thorisson was then living out at Raudamel. He had seven sons, and they were all promising men. Their names were Thorgils, Eyjolf and Thorir, and they were the leading men in that district.*

All the men who have been mentioned were living at the same time, and it was about this time that the best thing ever to have happened in Iceland occurred: the whole country became Christian and the entire population abandoned the old faith.

For six years now, Gunnlaug Serpent-tongue, who was mentioned earlier, had been living partly at Borg with Thorstein and partly at Gilsbakki with his father Illugi. By now, he was eighteen years old, and he and his father were getting on much better.

There was a man named Thorkel the Black. He was a member of Illugi's household and a close relative of his, and had grown up at Gilsbakki. He came into an inheritance at As in Vatnsdal up in the north, and asked Gunnlaug to go with him to collect it, which he did. They rode north to As together and, thanks to Gunnlaug's assistance, the men who had Thorkel's money handed it over to them.

On their way home from the north, they stayed overnight at Grimstungur with a wealthy farmer who was living there. In the morning, a shepherd took Gunnlaug's horse, which

---

* The copyist has presumably skipped a section in his exemplar, where the names of Thorfinn's four remaining sons were recorded.

was covered in sweat when they got it back. Gunnlaug knocked the shepherd senseless. The farmer would not leave it at that, and demanded compensation for the blow. Gunnlaug offered to pay him a mark, but the farmer thought that was too little. Then Gunnlaug spoke a verse:

1. A mark to the middle-strong man,
   lodgings-lord, I held out in my hand;   *lodgings-lord*: man
   you'll receive a fine silver-grey wire   *silver-grey wire*:
   for the one who spits flame from   piece of silver
     his gums.   *flame*: blood
   It will cause you regret
   if you knowingly let
   the sea-serpent's couch   *sea-serpent's couch*: gold
   slip out of your pouch.

They arranged that Gunnlaug's offer should be accepted, and when the matter was settled Gunnlaug and Thorkel rode home.

A little while later, Gunnlaug asked his father a second time for wares, so that he could travel abroad.

'Now you may have your own way,' Illugi replied, 'since you are better behaved than you used to be.'

Illugi rode off at once and bought Gunnlaug a half-share in a ship from Audun Halter-dog. The ship was beached in the Gufua estuary. This was the same Audun who, according to *The Saga of the People of Laxardal*, would not take the sons of Osvif the Wise abroad after the killing of Kjartan Olafsson, though that happened later than this.

When Illugi came home, Gunnlaug thanked him

profusely. Thorkel the Black went along with Gunnlaug, and their wares were loaded on to the ship. While the others were getting ready, Gunnlaug was at Borg, and he thought it was nicer to talk to Helga than to work with the traders.

One day, Thorstein asked Gunnlaug if he would like to ride up to his horses in Langavatnsdal with him. Gunnlaug said that he would, and they rode together until they arrived at Thorstein's shielings, which were at a place called Thorgilsstadir. Thorstein had a stud of four chestnut horses there. The stallion was a splendid creature, but was not an experienced fighter. Thorstein offered to give the horses to Gunnlaug, but he said that he did not need them, since he intended to go abroad. Then they rode over to another stud of horses. There was a grey stallion there with four mares; he was the best horse in Borgarfjord. Thorstein offered to give him to Gunnlaug.

'I don't want this horse any more than I wanted the others,' Gunnlaug answered. 'But why don't you offer me something I will accept?'

'What's that?' Thorstein asked.

'Your daughter, Helga the Fair,' Gunnlaug replied.

'That will not be arranged so swiftly,' he said, and changed the subject.

They rode home, down along the Langa river.

Then Gunnlaug spoke: 'I want to know how you will respond to my proposal.'

'I'm not taking any notice of your nonsense,' Thorstein replied.

'This is quite serious, and not nonsense,' Gunnlaug said.

'You should have worked out what you wanted in the

13

first place,' Thorstein countered. 'Haven't you decided to go abroad? And yet you're carrying on as if you want to get married. It wouldn't be suitable for you and Helga to marry while you are so undecided. I'm not prepared to consider it.'

'Where do you expect to find a match for your daughter if you won't marry her to Illugi the Black's son?' Gunnlaug asked. 'Where in Borgarfjord are there more important people than my father?'

'I don't go in for drawing comparisons between men,' Thorstein parried, 'but if you were such a man as he is you wouldn't be turned away.'

'To whom would you rather marry your daughter than me?' Gunnlaug asked.

'There's a lot of good men around here to choose from,' Thorstein replied. 'Thorfinn at Raudamel has seven sons, all of them very manly.'

'Neither Onund nor Thorfinn can compare with my father,' Gunnlaug answered, 'considering that even you clearly fall short of his mark. What have you done to compare with the time when he took on Thorgrim Kjallaksson the Godi and his sons at the Thorsnes Assembly by himself and came away with everything there was to be had?'

'I drove away Steinar, the son of Ogmund Sjoni – and that was considered quite an achievement,' Thorstein replied.

'You had your father, Egil, to help you then,' Gunnlaug retorted. 'Even so, there aren't many farmers who would be safe if they turned down a marriage bond with me.'

'You save your bullying for the people up in the hills,'

Thorstein replied. 'It won't count for much down here in the marshes.'

They arrived home later that evening, and the following morning Gunnlaug rode up to Gilsbakki and asked his father to ride back to Borg with him to make a marriage proposal.

'You are an unsettled fellow,' Illugi replied. 'You've already planned to go abroad, yet now you claim that you have to occupy yourself chasing after women. I know that Thorstein doesn't approve of such behaviour.'

'Nevertheless,' Gunnlaug replied, 'while I still intend to go abroad, nothing will please me unless you support me in this.'

Then Illugi rode down from Gilsbakki to Borg, taking eleven men with him. Thorstein gave them a warm welcome.

Early the next morning, Illugi said to Thorstein: 'I want to talk to you.'

'Let's go up on to the Borg* and talk there,' Thorstein suggested.

They did so, and Gunnlaug went along too.

Illugi spoke first: 'My kinsman Gunnlaug says that he has already spoken of this matter on his own behalf; he wants to ask for the hand of your daughter Helga. Now I want to know what is going to come of this. You know all about his breeding and our family's wealth. For our part, we will not

---

* The *Borg* is a high rocky outcrop immediately behind the site of Borg farm from which the farm takes its name.

neglect to provide either a farm or a godord, if that will help bring it about.'

'The only problem I have with Gunnlaug is that he seems so unsettled,' Thorstein replied. 'But if he were more like you, I shouldn't put it off.'

'If you deny that this would be an equal match for both our families, it will bring an end to our friendship,' Illugi warned.

'For our friendship's sake and because of what you've been saying, Helga will be promised to Gunnlaug, but not formally betrothed to him, and she will wait three years for him. And Gunnlaug must go abroad and follow the example of good men, and I will be free of any obligation if he doesn't come back as required, or if I don't like the way he turns out.'

With that, they parted. Illugi rode home and Gunnlaug rode off to his ship, and the merchants put to sea as soon as they got a fair wind. They sailed to the north of Norway, and then sailed in past Trondheim to Nidaros, where they berthed the ship and unloaded.

6   Earl Eirik Hakonarson and his brother Svein were ruling Norway in those days. Earl Eirik was staying on his family's estate at Lade, and was a powerful chieftain. Skuli Thorsteinsson was there with him: he was one of the earl's followers and was well thought of.

It is said that Gunnlaug and Audun Halter-dog went to Lade with ten other men. Gunnlaug was dressed in a grey tunic and white breeches. He had a boil on his foot, right on the instep, and blood and pus oozed out of it when he walked. In this state, he went before the earl with Audun and the others and greeted him politely. The earl recognized Audun, and asked him for news from Iceland, and Audun told him all there was. Then the earl asked Gunnlaug who he was, and Gunnlaug told him his name and what family he came from.

'Skuli Thorsteinsson,' the earl asked, 'what family does this fellow come from in Iceland?'

'My lord,' he replied, 'give him a good welcome. He is the son of the best man in Iceland, Illugi the Black from Gilsbakki, and, what's more, he's my foster-brother.'

'What's the matter with your foot, Icelander?' the earl asked.

'I've got a boil on it, my lord,' he replied.

'But you weren't limping?'

'One mustn't limp while both legs are the same length,' Gunnlaug replied.

Then a man named Thorir, who was one of the earl's followers, spoke: 'The Icelander is rather cocky. We should test him a bit.'

Gunnlaug looked at him, and spoke:

2. A certain follower's
   especially horrible;
   be wary of trusting him:
   he's evil and black.

Then Thorir made as if to grab his axe.

'Leave it be,' said the earl. 'Real men don't pay any attention to things like that. How old are you, Icelander?'

'Just turned eighteen,' Gunnlaug replied.

'I swear that you'll not survive another eighteen,' the earl declared.

'Don't you call curses down on me,' Gunnlaug muttered quite softly, 'but rather pray for yourself.'

'What did you just say, Icelander?' the earl asked.

'I said what I thought fit,' Gunnlaug replied, 'that you should not call curses down on me, but should pray more effective prayers for yourself.'

'What should I pray for then?' asked the earl.

'That you don't meet your death in the same way as your father Earl Hakon did.'*

The earl turned as red as blood, and ordered that the fool be arrested at once.

Then Skuli went to the earl and said, 'My lord, do as I ask: pardon the man and let him get out of here as quickly as he can.'

'Let him clear off as fast as he can if he wants quarter,' the earl commanded, 'and never set foot in my kingdom again.'

Then Skuli took Gunnlaug outside and down to the quay, where there was a ship all ready for its voyage to England. Skuli procured a passage in it for Gunnlaug and his kinsman Thorkel, and Gunnlaug entrusted his ship and the other belongings he did not need to keep with him to Audun for safe-keeping. Gunnlaug and Thorkel sailed off into the

---

* Earl Hakon Sigurdsson was murdered by his servant Kark, while hiding from his enemy Olaf Tryggvason in a pigsty.

North Sea, and arrived in the autumn at the port of London, where they drew the ship up on to its rollers.

7 King Ethelred, the son of Edgar, was ruling England at that time. He was a good ruler, and was spending that winter in London. In those days, the language in England was the same as that spoken in Norway and Denmark, but there was a change of language when William the Bastard conquered England. Since William was of French descent, the French language was used in England from then on.

As soon as he arrived in London, Gunnlaug went before the king and greeted him politely and respectfully. The king asked what country he was from. Gunnlaug told him – 'and I have come to you, my lord, because I have composed a poem about you, and I should like you to hear it'.

The king said that he would. Gunnlaug recited the poem expressively and confidently. The refrain goes like this:

3. All the army's in awe and agog
   at England's good prince, as at God:
   everyone lauds Ethelred the King,
   both the warlike king's race and men's kin.

The king thanked him for the poem and, as a reward, gave him a cloak of scarlet lined with the finest furs and with an embroidered band stretching down to the hem. He also made him one of his followers. Gunnlaug stayed with the king all winter and was well thought of.

Early one morning, Gunnlaug met three men in a street.

Their leader was named Thororm. He was big and strong, and rather obstreperous.

'Northerner,' he said, 'lend me some money.'

'It's not a good idea to lend money to strangers,' Gunnlaug replied.

'I'll pay you back on the date we agree between us,' he promised.

'I'll risk it then,' said Gunnlaug, giving Thororm the money.

A little while later, Gunnlaug met the king and told him about the loan.

'Now things have taken a turn for the worse,' the king replied. 'That fellow is the most notorious robber and thug. Have nothing more to do with him, and I will give you the same amount of money.'

'Then your followers are a pretty pathetic lot,' Gunnlaug answered. 'We trample all over innocent men, but let thugs like him walk all over us! That will never happen.'

Shortly afterwards, Gunnlaug met Thororm and demanded his money back, but Thororm said that he would not pay up. Then Gunnlaug spoke this verse:

4. O god of the sword-spell,
   you're unwise to withhold your wealth
   from me; you've deceived
   the sword-point's reddener.
   I've something else to explain –
   'Serpent-tongue' as a child
   was my name. Now again
   here's my chance to prove why.

sword-spell: battle; its *god*: warrior

sword-point's reddener: warrior, who reddens the sword's point with blood

'Now I'll give you the choice the law provides for,' said Gunnlaug. 'Either you pay me my money or fight a duel with me in three days' time.'

The thug laughed and said, 'Many people have suffered badly at my hands, and no one has ever challenged me to a duel before. I'm quite ready for it!'

With that, Gunnlaug and Thororm parted for the time being. Gunnlaug told the king how things stood.

'Now we really are in a fix,' he said. 'This man can blunt any weapon just by looking at it. You must do exactly as I tell you. I am going to give you this sword, and you are to fight him with it, but make sure that you show him a different one.'

Gunnlaug thanked the king warmly.

When they were ready for the duel, Thororm asked Gunnlaug what kind of sword he happened to have. Gunnlaug showed him and drew the sword, but he had fastened a loop of rope around the hilt of King's Gift and he slipped it over his wrist.

As soon as he saw the sword, the berserk said, 'I'm not afraid of that sword.'

He struck at Gunnlaug with his sword, and chopped off most of his shield. Then Gunnlaug struck back with his sword King's Gift. The berserk left himself exposed, because he thought Gunnlaug was using the same weapon as he had shown him. Gunnlaug dealt him his death-blow there and then. The king thanked him for this service, and Gunnlaug won great fame for it in England and beyond.

In the spring, when ships were sailing from country to country, Gunnlaug asked Ethelred for permission to do some travelling. The king asked him what he wanted to do.

'I should like to fulfil a vow I have made,' Gunnlaug answered, and spoke this verse:

5. I will most surely visit
   three shapers of war   *shapers of war*: kings
   and two earls of lands,
   as I promised worthy men.
   I will not be back
   before the point-goddess's son   *point-goddess*: valkyrie; her *son*:
   summons me; he gives me   Ethelred
   a red serpent's bed to wear.   *serpent's bed*: gold

'And so it will be, poet,' said the king, giving him a gold arm ring weighing six ounces. 'But,' he continued, 'you must promise to come back to me next autumn, because I don't want to lose such an accomplished man as you.'

8   Then Gunnlaug sailed north to Dublin with some merchants. At that time, Ireland was ruled by King Sigtrygg Silk-beard, the son of Olaf Kvaran and Queen Kormlod. He had only been king for a short while. Straight away, Gunnlaug went before the king and greeted him politely and respectfully. The king gave him an honourable welcome.

'I have composed a poem about you,' Gunnlaug said, 'and I should like it to have a hearing.'

'No one has ever deigned to bring me a poem before,' the king replied. 'Of course I will listen to it.'

Gunnlaug recited the drapa, and the refrain goes like this:

6. To the sorceress's steed   *sorceress's steed*: wolf
   Sigtrygg corpses feeds.

And it contains these lines as well:

7. I know which offspring,
   descendant of kings,
   I want to proclaim
   – Kvaran's son is his name;
   it is his habit
   to be quite lavish:
   the poet's ring of gold
   he surely won't withhold.

8. The flinger of Frodi's flame   *Frodi's* (sea-king's) *flame*: gold; its
   should eloquently explain   *flinger*: generous man (Sigtrygg)
   if he's found phrasing neater
   than mine, in drapa metre.

The king thanked Gunnlaug for the poem, and summoned his treasurer.

'How should I reward the poem?' he asked.

'How would you like to, my lord?' the treasurer said.

'What kind of reward would it be if I gave him a pair of knorrs?' the king asked.

'That is too much, my lord,' he replied. 'Other kings give fine treasures – good swords or splendid gold bracelets – as rewards for poems.'

The king gave Gunnlaug his own new suit of scarlet

clothes, an embroidered tunic, a cloak lined with exquisite furs and a gold bracelet which weighed a mark. Gunnlaug thanked him profusely and stayed there for a short while. He went on from there to the Orkney Islands.

In those days, the Orkney Islands were ruled by Earl Sigurd Hlodvesson. He thought highly of Icelanders. Gunnlaug greeted the earl politely and said that he had a poem to present to him. The earl said that he would indeed listen to Gunnlaug's poem, since he was from such an important family in Iceland. Gunnlaug recited the poem, which was a well-constructed flokk. As a reward, the earl gave him a broad axe, decorated all over with silver inlay, and invited Gunnlaug to stay with him.

Gunnlaug thanked him for the gift, and for the invitation, too, but said that he had to travel east to Sweden. Then he took passage with some merchants who were sailing to Norway, and that autumn they arrived at Kungalf in the east. As always, Gunnlaug's kinsman, Thorkel, was still with him. They took a guide from Kungalf up into Vastergotland and so arrived at the market town named Skarar. An earl named Sigurd, who was rather old, was ruling there. Gunnlaug went before him and greeted him politely, saying that he had composed a poem about him. The earl listened carefully as Gunnlaug recited the poem, which was a flokk. Afterwards, the earl thanked Gunnlaug, rewarded him generously and asked him to stay with him over the winter.

Earl Sigurd held a great Yule feast during the winter. Messengers from Earl Eirik arrived on Yule eve. They had travelled down from Norway. There were twelve of them in all, and they were bearing gifts for Earl Sigurd. The earl gave them a warm welcome and seated them next to Gunnlaug for the Yule festival. There was a great deal of merriment. The people of Vastergotland declared that there was no better or more famous earl than Sigurd; the Norwegians thought that Earl Eirik was much better. They argued about this and, in the end, both sides called upon Gunnlaug to settle the matter. It was then that Gunnlaug spoke this verse:

9. Staves of the spear-sister,
   you speak of the earl:
   this old man is hoary-haired,
   but has looked on tall waves.
   Before his billow-steed
   battle-bush Eirik, tossed
   by the tempest, has seen
   more blue breakers back in the east.

spear-sister: valkyrie; her *staves*: warriors

billow-steed: ship
battle-bush: warrior

Both sides, but particularly the Norwegians, were pleased with this assessment. After Yule, the messengers left with splendid gifts from Earl Sigurd to Earl Eirik. They told Earl Eirik about Gunnlaug's assessment. The earl thought that Gunnlaug had shown him both fairness and friendliness, and spread the word that Gunnlaug would find a safe haven in his domain. Gunnlaug later heard what the earl had had to say about the matter. Gunnlaug had asked Earl Sigurd for a guide to take him east into Tiundaland in Sweden, and the earl found him one.

9   In those days, Sweden was ruled by King Olaf the
    Swede, the son of King Eirik the Victorious and Sigrid
the Ambitious, daughter of Tosti the Warlike. He was a
powerful and illustrious king, and was very keen to make
his mark.

Gunnlaug arrived in Uppsala around the time of the
Swedes' Spring Assembly. When he managed to get an audi-
ence, he greeted the king, who welcomed him warmly and
asked him who he was. He said that he was an Icelander.
Now Hrafn Onundarson was with the king at the time.

'Hrafn,' the king said, 'what family does this fellow come
from in Iceland?'

A big, dashing man stood up from the lower bench, came
before the king and said, 'My lord, he comes from the finest
of families and is the noblest of men in his own right.'

'Then let him go and sit next to you,' the king said.

'I have a poem to present to you,' Gunnlaug said, 'and I
should like you to listen to it properly.'

'First go and sit yourselves down,' the king commanded.
'There is no time now to sit and listen to poems.'

And so they did. Gunnlaug and Hrafn started to chat,
telling one another about their travels. Hrafn said that he
had left Iceland for Norway the previous summer, and had
come east to Sweden early that winter. They were soon good
friends.

One day when the assembly was over, Hrafn and Gunnlaug were both there with the king.

'Now, my lord,' Gunnlaug said, 'I should like you to hear
my poem.'

'I could do that now,' the king replied.

'I want to recite my poem now, my lord,' Hrafn said.

'I could listen to that, too,' he replied.

'I want to recite my poem first,' Gunnlaug said, 'if you please.'

'I should go first, my lord,' Hrafn said, 'since I came to your court first.'

'Where did our ancestors ever go with mine trailing in the wake of yours?' Gunnlaug asked. 'Nowhere, that's where! And that's how it's going to be with us, too!'

'Let's be polite enough not to fight over this,' Hrafn replied. 'Let's ask the king to decide.'

'Gunnlaug had better recite his poem first,' the king declared, 'since he takes it badly if he doesn't get his own way.'

Then Gunnlaug recited the drapa he had composed about King Olaf, and when he had finished, the king said, 'How well is the poem composed, Hrafn?'

'Quite well, my lord,' he answered. 'It is an ostentatious poem, but is ungainly and rather stilted, just like Gunnlaug himself is in temperament.'

'Now you must recite your poem, Hrafn,' the king said.

He did so, and when he had finished, the king asked: 'How well is the poem put together, Gunnlaug?'

'Quite well, my lord,' he replied. 'It is a handsome poem, just like Hrafn himself is, but there's not much to either of them. And,' he continued, 'why did you compose only a flokk for the king, Hrafn? Did you not think he merited a drapa?'

'Let's not talk about this any farther,' Hrafn said. 'It might well crop up again later.' And with that they parted.

A little while later, Hrafn was made one of King Olaf's followers. He asked for permission to leave, which the king granted.

Now when Hrafn was ready to leave, he said to Gunnlaug, 'From now on, our friendship is over, since you tried to do me down in front of the court. Sometime soon, I will cause you no less shame than you tried to heap on me here.'

'Your threats don't scare me,' Gunnlaug replied, 'and I won't be thought a lesser man than you anywhere.'

King Olaf gave Hrafn valuable gifts when they parted, and then Hrafn went away.

Hrafn left the east that spring and went to Trondheim, where he fitted out his ship. He sailed to Iceland during the summer, and brought his ship into Leiruvog, south of Mosfell heath. His family and friends were glad to see him, and he stayed at home with his father over the winter.

Now at the Althing that summer, Hrafn the Poet met his kinsman Skafti the Lawspeaker.

'I should like you to help me ask Thorstein Egilsson for permission to marry his daughter Helga,' Hrafn said.

'Hasn't she already been promised to Gunnlaug Serpent-tongue?' Skafti answered.

'Hasn't the time they agreed passed by now?' Hrafn countered. 'Besides, Gunnlaug's so proud these days that he won't take any notice of this or care about it all.'

'We'll do as you please,' Skafti replied.

Then they went over to Thorstein Egilsson's booth with several other men. Thorstein gave them a warm welcome.

'My kinsman Hrafn wants to ask for the hand of your daughter Helga,' Skafti explained. 'You know about his family background, his wealth and good breeding, and that he has numerous relatives and friends.'

'She is already promised to Gunnlaug,' Thorstein answered, 'and I want to stick to every detail of the agreement I made with him.'

'Haven't the three winters you agreed between yourselves passed by now?' Skafti asked.

'Yes,' said Thorstein, 'but the summer isn't gone, and he might yet come back during the summer.'

'But if he hasn't come back at the end of the summer, then what hope will we have in the matter?' Skafti asked.

'We'll all come back here next summer,' Thorstein replied, 'and then we'll be able to see what seems to be the best way forward, but there's no point in talking about it any more at the moment.'

With that they parted, and people rode home from the Althing. It was no secret that Hrafn had asked for Helga's hand.

Gunnlaug did not return that summer. At the Althing the next summer, Skafti and Hrafn argued their case vehemently, saying that Thorstein was now free of all his obligations to Gunnlaug.

'I don't have many daughters to look after,' Thorstein said, 'and I'm anxious that no one be provoked to violence on their account. Now I want to see Illugi the Black first.'

And so he did.

When Illugi and Thorstein met, Thorstein asked, 'Do you

consider me to be free of all obligation to your son Gunnlaug?'

'Certainly,' Illugi replied, 'if that's how you want it. I cannot add much to this now, because I don't altogether know what Gunnlaug's circumstances are.'

Then Thorstein went back to Skafti. They settled matters by deciding that, if Gunnlaug did not come back that summer, Hrafn and Helga's marriage should take place at Borg at the Winter Nights, but that Thorstein should be without obligation to Hrafn if Gunnlaug were to come back and go through with the wedding. After that, people rode home from the Althing. Gunnlaug's return was still delayed, and Helga did not like the arrangement at all.

10 Now we return to Gunnlaug, who left Sweden for England in the same summer as Hrafn went back to Iceland. He received valuable gifts from King Olaf when he left. King Ethelred gave Gunnlaug a very warm welcome. He stayed with the king all winter, and was thought well of.

In those days, the ruler of Denmark was Canute the Great, the son of Svein. He had recently come into his inheritance, and was continually threatening to lead an army against England, since his father, Svein, had gained considerable power in England before his death there in the west. Furthermore, there was a huge army of Danes in Britain at that time. Its leader was Heming, the son of Earl Strut-Harald and the brother of Earl Sigvaldi. Under King Canute, Heming was in charge of the territory which King Svein had previously won.

During the spring, Gunnlaug asked King Ethelred for permission to leave.

'Since you are my follower,' he replied, 'it is not appropriate for you to leave me when such a war threatens England.'

'That is for you to decide, my lord,' Gunnlaug replied. 'But give me permission to leave next summer, if the Danes don't come.'

'We'll see about it then,' the king answered.

Now that summer and the following winter passed, and the Danes did not come. After midsummer, Gunnlaug obtained the king's permission to leave, went east to Norway and visited Earl Eirik at Lade in Trondheim. The earl gave him a warm welcome this time, and invited him to stay with him. Gunnlaug thanked him for the offer, but said that he wanted to go back to Iceland first, to visit his intended.

'All the ships prepared for Iceland are gone now,' said the earl.

Then a follower said, 'Hallfred the Troublesome Poet was still anchored out under Agdenes yesterday.'

'That might still be the case,' the earl replied. 'He sailed from here five nights ago.'

Then Earl Eirik had Gunnlaug taken out to Hallfred, who was glad to see him. An offshore breeze began to blow, and they were very cheerful. It was late summer.

'Have you heard about Hrafn Onundarson's asking for permission to marry Helga the Fair?' Hallfred asked Gunnlaug.

Gunnlaug said that he had heard about it, but that he did not know the full story. Hallfred told him everything he knew about it, and added that many people said that Hrafn might well prove to be no less brave than Gunnlaug was. Then Gunnlaug spoke this verse:

10. Though the east wind has toyed
with the shore-ski this week   *shore-ski*: ship
I weigh that but little –
the weather's weaker now.
I fear more being felt
to fall short of Hrafn in courage
than living on to become
a grey-haired gold-breaker.   *gold-breaker*: man

Then Hallfred said, 'You will need to have better dealings with Hrafn than I did. A few years ago, I brought my ship into Leiruvog, south of Mosfell heath. I ought to have paid Hrafn's farmhand half a mark of silver, but I didn't give it to him. Hrafn rode over to us with sixty men and cut our mooring ropes, and the ship drifted up on to the mud flats and looked as if it would be wrecked. I ended up granting Hrafn self-judgement, and paid him a mark. That is all I have to say about him.'

From then on, they talked only about Helga. Hallfred heaped much praise on her beauty. Then Gunnlaug spoke:

11. The slander-wary god
    of the sword-storm's spark

sword-storm: battle; *its spark*:
sword; *god*

mustn't court the cape of the earth
with her cover of linen like snow.

of the sword: warrior(Hrafn)

For when I was a lad,
I played on the headlands
of the forearm's fire
with that land-fishes' bed-land.

forearm's fire: ring; its
headlands: fingers;
played on the fingers: was
her favourite
(*or* caressed her)
land-fishes: snakes; their *beds*:
gold; gold-*land*: woman

'That is well composed,' Hallfred said.

They came ashore at Hraunhofn on Melrakkasletta a fortnight before winter, and unloaded the ship.

There was a man named Thord, who was the son of the farmer on Melrakkasletta. He was always challenging the merchants at wrestling, and they generally came off worse against him. Then a bout was arranged between him and Gunnlaug, and the night before, Thord called upon Thor to bring him victory. When they met the next day, they began to wrestle. Gunnlaug swept both Thord's legs out from under him, and his opponent fell down hard, but Gunnlaug twisted his own ankle out of joint when he put his weight on that leg, and he fell down with Thord.

'Maybe your next fight won't go any better,' Thord said.

'What do you mean?' Gunnlaug asked.

'I'm talking about the quarrel you'll be having with Hrafn

33

when he marries Helga the Fair at the Winter Nights. I was there when it was arranged at the Althing this summer.'

Gunnlaug did not reply. Then his foot was bandaged and the joint reset. It was badly swollen.

Hallfred and Gunnlaug rode south with ten other men, and arrived at Gilsbakki in Borgarfjord on the same Saturday evening that the others were sitting down to the wedding feast at Borg. Illugi was glad to see his son Gunnlaug and his companions. Gunnlaug said that he wanted to ride down to Borg there and then, but Illugi said that this was not wise. Everyone else thought so too, except Gunnlaug, but he was incapacitated by his foot – although he did not let it show – and so the journey did not take place. In the morning, Hallfred rode home to Hreduvatn in Nordurardal. His brother Galti, who was a splendid fellow, was looking after their property there.

11   Now we turn to Hrafn, who was sitting down to his wedding feast at Borg. Most people say that the bride was rather gloomy. It is true that, as the saying goes, 'things learned young last longest', and that was certainly the case with her just then.

It so happened that a man named Sverting, who was the son of Goat-Bjorn, the son of Molda-Gnup, asked for the hand of Hungerd, the daughter of Thorodd and Jofrid. The wedding was to take place up at Skaney later in the winter, after Yule. A relative of Hungerd's, Thorkel the son of Torfi Valbrandsson, lived at Skaney. Torfi's mother was Thorodda, the sister of Tunga-Odd.

Hrafn went home to Mosfell with his wife Helga. One morning, when they had been living there for a little while,

Helga was lying awake before they got up, but Hrafn was still sleeping. His sleep was rather fitful, and when he woke up, Helga asked him what he had been dreaming about. Then Hrafn spoke this verse:

12. I thought I'd been stabbed
    by a yew of serpent's dew   *serpent's dew*: blood;
    and with my blood, O my bride,   its *yew* (twig): sword
    your bed was stained red.
    Beer-bowl's goddess, you weren't   *beer-bowl's goddess*:
    able to bind up the damage   woman (Helga)
    that the drubbing-thorn dealt to Hrafn: *drubbing-thorn*: sword
    linden of herbs, that might please you.   *linden* (tree) *of herbs*:
        woman

'I will never weep over that,' Helga said. 'You have all tricked me wickedly. Gunnlaug must have come back.' And then Helga wept bitterly.

Indeed, a little while later news came of Gunnlaug's return. After this, Helga grew so intractable towards Hrafn that he could not keep her at home, and so they went back to Borg. Hrafn did not enjoy much intimacy with her.

Now people were making plans for the winter's other wedding. Thorkel from Skaney invited Illugi the Black and his sons. But while Illugi was getting ready, Gunnlaug sat in the main room and did not make any move towards getting ready himself.

Illugi went up to him and said, 'Why aren't you getting ready, son?'

'I don't intend to go,' Gunnlaug replied.

35

'Of course you will go, son,' Illugi said. 'And don't set so much store by yearning for just one woman. Behave as though you haven't noticed, and you'll never be short of women.'

Gunnlaug did as his father said, and they went to the feast. Illugi and his sons were given one high seat, and Thorstein Egilsson, his son-in-law Hrafn and the bridegroom's group had the other one, opposite Illugi. The women were sitting on the cross-bench, and Helga the Fair was next to the bride. She often cast her eyes in Gunnlaug's direction, and so it was proved that, as the saying goes, 'if a woman loves a man, her eyes won't hide it'. Gunnlaug was well turned out, and had on the splendid clothes which King Sigtrygg had given him. He seemed far superior to other men for many reasons, what with his strength, his looks and his figure.

People did not particularly enjoy the wedding feast. On the same day as the men were getting ready to leave, the women started to break up their party, too, and began getting themselves ready for the journey home. Gunnlaug went to talk to Helga, and they chatted for a long time. Then Gunnlaug spoke this verse:

13. For Serpent-tongue no full day
    under mountains' hall was easy   *mountains' hall*: sky
    since Helga the Fair
    took the name of Hrafn's Wife.
    But her father, white-faced
    wielder of whizzing spears,
    took no heed of my tongue.
    – the goddess was married for money.

And he spoke another one, too:

14. Fair wine-goddess, I must reward   *wine-goddess*: woman
    your father for the worst wound –   (Helga)
    the land of the flood-flame steals joy   *flood-flame*: gold; its
    from this poet – and also your mother.   *land*: woman
    For beneath bedclothes they both
    made a band-goddess so beautiful: *band-goddess*: woman
    the devil take the handiwork   wearing garments of
    of that bold man and woman!   woven bands (Helga)

And then Gunnlaug gave Helga the cloak Ethelred had given him, which was very splendid. She thanked him sincerely for the gift.

Then Gunnlaug went outside. By now, mares and stallions – many of them fine animals – had been led into the yard, saddled up and tethered there. Gunnlaug leapt on to one of the stallions and rode at a gallop across the hayfield to where Hrafn was standing. Hrafn had to duck out of his way.

'There's no need to duck, Hrafn,' Gunnlaug said, 'because I don't mean to do you any harm at the moment, though you know what you deserve.'

Hrafn answered with this verse:

15. Glorifier of battle-goddess,   *battle-goddess*: valkyrie; her
   god of the quick-flying weapon,   *glorifier*: warrior;
   it's not fitting for us to fight   *god of the . . . weapon*: warrior
   over one fair tunic-goddess.   *tunic-goddess*: woman
   Slaughter-tree, south over sea   *Slaughter-tree*. warrior
   there are many such women,
   you will rest assured of that.
   I set my wave-steed to sail.   *wave-steed*: ship

'There may well be a lot of women,' Gunnlaug replied,
'but it doesn't look that way to me.'

Then Illugi and Thorstein ran over to them, and would
not let them fight each other. Gunnlaug spoke a verse:

16. The fresh-faced goddess
   of the serpent's day   *serpent's day* (i.e.
   was handed to Hrafn for pay –   brightness): gold;
   he's equal to me, people say –   its *goddess*: woman
   while in the pounding of steel   *pounding of steel*: battle
   peerless Ethelred delayed
   my journey from the east – that's why
   the jewel-foe's less greedy for words.   *jewel-foe*: generous
                       man (Gunnlaug)

After that, both parties went home, and nothing worth
mentioning happened all winter. Hrafn never again enjoyed
intimacy with Helga after she and Gunnlaug had met once
more.

That summer, people made their way to the Althing in
large groups: Illugi the Black took his sons Gunnlaug and

Hermund with him; Thorstein Egilsson took his son Kolls-vein; Onund from Mosfell took all his sons; and Sverting the son of Goat-Bjorn also went. Skafti was still Lawspeaker then.

One day during the Althing, when people were thronging to the Law Rock and the legal business was done, Gunnlaug demanded a hearing and said, 'Is Hrafn Onundarson here?'

Hrafn said that he was.

Then Gunnlaug Serpent-tongue said, 'You know that you have married my intended and have drawn yourself into enmity with me because of it. Now I challenge you to a duel to take place here at the Althing in three days' time on Oxa-rarholm (Axe River Island).'

'That's a fine-sounding challenge,' Hrafn replied, 'as might be expected from you. Whenever you like – I'm quite ready for it!'

Both sets of relatives were upset by this, but, in those days, the law said that anyone who felt he'd received under-hand treatment from someone else could challenge him to a duel.

Now when the three days were up, they got themselves ready for the duel. Illugi the Black went to the island with his son, along with a large body of men; and Skafti the Law-speaker went with Hrafn, as did his father and other relatives. Before Gunnlaug went out on to the island, he spoke this verse:

17. I'm ready to tread the isle
    where combat is tried
    – God grant the poet victory –
    a drawn sword in my hand;
    into two I'll slice the hair-seat   *hair-seat*: head
    of Helga's kiss-gulper;   *Helga's kiss-gulper*: her lover,
    finally, with my bright sword,   Hrafn
    I'll unscrew his head from his neck.

Hrafn replied with this one:

18. The poet doesn't know
    which poet will rejoice –
    wound-sickles are drawn,   *wound-sickles*: swords
    the edge fit to bite leg.
    Both single and a widow,
    from the Thing the thorn-tray will hear   *thorns*: brooch-pins,
    – though bloodied I might be –   its *tray*: woman
    tales of her man's bravery.

Hermund held his brother Gunnlaug's shield for him; and
Sverting, Goat-Bjorn's son, held Hrafn's. Whoever was
wounded was to pay three marks of silver to release himself
from the duel. Hrafn was to strike the first blow, since he
had been challenged. He hacked at the top of Gunnlaug's
shield, and the blow was so mightily struck that the sword
promptly broke off below the hilt. The point of the sword
glanced up and caught Gunnlaug on the cheek, scratching
him slightly. Straight away, their fathers, along with several
other people, ran between them.

Then Gunnlaug said, 'I submit that Hrafn is defeated, because he is weaponless.'

'And I submit that you are defeated,' Hrafn replied, 'because you have been wounded.'

Gunnlaug got very angry and said, all in a rage, that the matter had not been resolved. Then his father, Illugi, said that there should not be any more resolving for the moment.

'Next time Hrafn and I meet, Father,' Gunnlaug said, 'I should like you to be too far away to separate us.'

With that they parted for the time being, and everyone went back to their booths.

Now the following day, it was laid down as law by the Law Council that all duelling should be permanently abolished. This was done on the advice of all the wisest men at the Althing, and all the wisest men in Iceland were there. Thus the duel which Hrafn and Gunnlaug fought was the last one ever to take place in Iceland. This was one of the three most-crowded Althings of all time, the others being the one after the burning of Njal and the one following the Slayings on the Heath.

One morning, when the brothers Hermund and Gunnlaug were on their way to the Oxara river to wash themselves, several women were going to its opposite bank. Helga the Fair was one of them.

Then Hermund asked Gunnlaug, 'Can you see your girl-friend Helga on the other side of the river?'

'Of course I can see her,' Gunnlaug replied. And then he spoke this verse:

19. The woman was born to bring war
    between men – the tree of the valkyrie
    started it all; I wanted her
    sorely, that log of rare silver.
    Henceforward, my black eyes
    are scarcely of use to glance
    at the ring-land's light-goddess,
    splendid as a swan.

tree of the valkyrie: warrior (perhaps Hrafn, but more probably Thorstein)
log of silver: woman
ring-land: hand; its
light: ring;
goddess of the ring: woman

Then they went across the river, and Helga and Gunnlaug chatted for a while. When they went back eastwards across the river, Helga stood and stared at Gunnlaug for a long time. Then Gunnlaug looked back across the river and spoke this verse:

20. The moon of her eyelash – that valkyrie
    adorned with linen, server of herb-surf,
    shone hawk-sharp upon me
    beneath her brow's bright sky;
    but that beam from the eyelid-moon
    of the goddess of the golden torque
    will later bring trouble to me
    and to the ring-goddess herself.

moon: eye
herb-surf: ale; its
server: woman
brow's sky: forehead
beam: gaze
goddess of the golden torque: woman
ring-goddess: woman

After this had happened, everyone rode home from the Althing, and Gunnlaug settled down at home at Gilsbakki. One morning, when he woke up, everyone was up and about except him. He slept in a bed closet further into the hall than were the benches. Then twelve men, all armed to the teeth, came into the hall: Hrafn Onundarson had arrived. Gunnlaug leapt up with a start, and managed to grab his weapons.

'You're not in any danger,' Hrafn said, 'and you'll hear what brings me here right now. You challenged me to a duel at the Althing last summer, and you thought that the matter was not fully resolved. Now I want to suggest that we both leave Iceland this summer and travel to Norway and fight a duel over there. Our relatives won't be able to stand between us there.'

'Well spoken, man!' Gunnlaug replied. 'I accept your proposal with pleasure. And now, Hrafn, you may have whatever hospitality you would like here.'

'That is a kind offer,' Hrafn replied, 'but, for the moment, we must ride on our way.'

And with that they parted. Both sets of relatives were very upset about this, but, because of their own anger, they could do nothing about it. But what fate decreed must come to pass.

12 Now we return to Hrafn. He fitted out his ship in Leiruvog. The names of two men who travelled with him are known: they were the sons of his father Onund's sister, one named Grim and the other Olaf. They were both worthy men. All Hrafn's relatives thought it was a great blow when he went away, but he explained that he had challenged Gunnlaug to a duel because he was not getting anywhere with Helga; one of them, he said, would have to perish at the hands of the other.

Hrafn set sail when he got a fair breeze, and they brought the ship to Trondheim, where he spent the winter. He received no news of Gunnlaug that winter, and so he waited there for him all summer, and then spent yet another winter in Trondheim at a place named Levanger.

Gunnlaug Serpent-tongue sailed from Melrakkasletta in the north with Hallfred the Troublesome Poet. They left their preparations very late, and put to sea as soon as they got a fair breeze, arriving in the Orkney Islands shortly before winter.

The islands were ruled by Earl Sigurd Hlodvesson at that time, and Gunnlaug went to him and spent the winter there. He was well respected. During the spring, the earl got ready to go plundering. Gunnlaug made preparations to go with him, and they spent the summer plundering over a large part of the Hebrides and the Scottish firths and fought many battles. Wherever they went, Gunnlaug proved himself to be a very brave and valiant fellow, and very manly. Earl Sigurd turned back in the early part of the summer, and then Gunnlaug took passage with some merchants who were sailing to Norway. Gunnlaug and Earl Sigurd parted on very friendly terms.

Gunnlaug went north to Lade in Trondheim to visit Earl Eirik, arriving at the beginning of winter. The earl gave him a warm welcome, and invited him to stay with him. Gunnlaug accepted the invitation. The earl had already heard about the goings-on between Gunnlaug and Hrafn, and he told Gunnlaug that he would not allow them to fight in his realm. Gunnlaug said that such matters were for the earl to decide. He stayed there that winter, and was always rather withdrawn.

Now one day that spring, Gunnlaug and his kinsman Thorkel went out for a walk. They headed away from the town, and in the fields in front of them was a ring of men. Inside the ring, two armed men were fencing. One had been given the name Gunnlaug, and the other one Hrafn. The bystanders said that Icelanders struck out with mincing blows and were slow to remember their promises. Gunnlaug realized that there was a great deal of contempt in this, that it was a focus for mockery, and he went away in silence.

A little while after this, Gunnlaug told the earl that he did not feel inclined to put up with his followers' contempt and mockery concerning the goings-on between himself and Hrafn any longer. He asked the earl to provide him with guides to Levanger. The earl had already been told that Hrafn had left Levanger and gone across into Sweden, and he therefore gave Gunnlaug permission to go, and found him two guides for the journey.

Then Gunnlaug left Lade with six other men, and went to Levanger. He arrived during the evening, but Hrafn had departed from there with four men the same morning. Gunnlaug went from there into Veradal, always arriving in the evening at the place where Hrafn had been the night before. Gunnlaug pressed on until he reached the innermost farm in the valley, which was named Sula, but Hrafn had left there that morning. Gunnlaug did not break his journey there, however, but pressed on through the night, and they caught sight of each other at sunrise the next day. Hrafn had reached a place where there were two lakes, with a stretch of flat land between them. This area was named Gleipnisvellir (Gleipnir's Plains). A small headland called Dingenes jutted out into one of the lakes. Hrafn's party, which was five strong, took up position on the headland. His kinsmen, Grim and Olaf, were with him.

When they met, Gunnlaug said, 'It's good that we have met now.'

Hrafn said that he had no problem with it himself – 'and now you must choose which you prefer,' he said. 'Either we will all fight, or just the two of us, but both sides must be equal.'

Gunnlaug said that he would be quite happy with either arrangement. Then Hrafn's kinsmen, Grim and Olaf, said that they would not stand by while Gunnlaug and Hrafn fought. Thorkel the Black, Gunnlaug's kinsman, said the same.

Then Gunnlaug told the earl's guides: 'You must sit by and help neither side, and be there to tell the story of our encounter.' And so they did.

Then they fell to, and everyone fought bravely. Grim and Olaf together attacked Gunnlaug alone, and the business between them ended in his killing them both, though he was not himself hurt. Thord Kolbeinsson confirms this in the poem he composed about Gunnlaug Serpent-tongue:

21. Before reaching Hrafn,
    Gunnlaug hacked down Grim
    and Olaf, men pleased
    with the valkyrie's warm wind;   *valkyrie's warm wind*: battle
    blood-bespattered, the brave one
    was the bane of three bold men;
    the god of the wave-charger   *wave-charger*: ship; its *god*:
    dealt death out to men.   seafarer, man

Meanwhile, Hrafn and Thorkel the Black, Gunnlaug's kinsman, were fighting. Thorkel succumbed to Hrafn, and lost his life. In the end, all their companions fell. Then the two of them, Hrafn and Gunnlaug, fought on, setting about each other remorselessly with heavy blows and fearless counter-attacks. Gunnlaug was using the sword which Ethelred had given him, and it was a formidable weapon. In the end, he hacked at Hrafn with a mighty blow, and chopped off his leg. Yet Hrafn did not collapse completely, but dropped back to a tree stump and rested the stump of his leg on it.

'Now you're past fighting,' Gunnlaug said, 'and I will not fight with you, a wounded man, any longer.'

'It is true that things have turned against me, rather,' Hrafn replied, 'but I should be able to hold out all right if I could get something to drink.'

'Don't trick me then,' Gunnlaug replied, 'if I bring you water in my helmet.'

'I won't trick you,' Hrafn said.

Then Gunnlaug went to a brook, fetched some water in his helmet and took it to Hrafn. But as Hrafn reached out his left hand for it, he hacked at Gunnlaug's head with the sword in his right hand, causing a hideous wound.

'Now you have cruelly deceived me,' Gunnlaug said, 'and you have behaved in an unmanly way, since I trusted you.'

'That is true,' Hrafn replied, 'and I did it because I would not have you receive the embrace of Helga the Fair.'

Then they fought fiercely again, and it finished in Gunnlaug's over-powering Hrafn, and Hrafn lost his life right there. Then the earl's guides went over and bound Gunnlaug's head wound. He sat still throughout and spoke this verse:

22. Hrafn, that bold sword-swinger,
     splendid sword-meeting's tree,   *sword-meeting*: battle; its *tree*:
     in the harsh storm of stingers   warrior
     advanced bravely against me.   *stingers*: spears; *spears' storm*:
     This morning, many metal-flights   battle
     howled round Gunnlaug's head   *metal-flights*: thrown
     on Dingenes, O ring-birch   weapons
     and protector of ranks.   *ring-birch*: man
                                                               protector of ranks: leader of
                                                               an army, warrior

Then they saw to the dead men, and afterwards they put Gunnlaug on his horse and brought him down into Levanger. There he lay for three nights, and received the full rites from a priest before he died. He was buried in the church there. Everyone thought the deaths of both Gunnlaug and Hrafn in such circumstances were a great loss.

13 That summer, before this news had been heard out here in Iceland, Illugi the Black had a dream. He was at home at Gilsbakki at the time. He dreamed that Gunnlaug appeared to him, covered in blood, and spoke this verse to him. Illugi remembered the poem when he woke up, and later recited it to other people:

23. I know that Hrafn hit me
    with the hilt-finned fish
    that hammers on mail,
    but my sharp edge bit his leg
    when the eagle, corpse-scorer,
    drank the mead of warm wounds.
    The war-twig of valkyrie's thorns
    split Gunnlaug's skull.

fish: sword (with a hilt for fins)
corpse-scorer: eagle, which carves up corpses with its beak
mead of wounds: blood
valkyrie's thorns: warriors; their *war-twig*: sword

On the same night, at Mosfell in the south, it happened that Onund dreamed that Hrafn came to him. He was all covered in blood, and spoke this verse:

24. My sword was stained with gore,
    but the Odin of swords
    sword-swiped me too; on shields
    shield-giants were tried overseas.
    I think there stood blood-stained
    blood-goslings in blood round my brain.
    Once more the wound-eager wound-raven
    wound-river is fated to wade.

Odin (god) *of swords*: warrior (Gunnlaug)
shield-giants: enemies of shields, i.e. swords
blood-goslings: ravens
wound-river: blood

49

At the Althing the following summer, Illugi the Black spoke to Onund at the Law Rock.

'How are you going to compensate me for my son,' he asked, 'since your son Hrafn tricked him when they had declared a truce?'

'I don't think there's any onus on me to pay compensation for him,' Onund replied, 'since I've been so sorely wounded by their encounter myself. But I won't ask you for any compensation for my son, either.'

'Then some of your family and friends will suffer for it,' Illugi answered. And all summer, after the Althing, Illugi was very depressed.

People say that during the autumn, Illugi rode off from Gilsbakki with about thirty men, and arrived at Mosfell early in the morning. Onund and his sons rushed into the church, but Illugi captured two of Onund's kinsmen. One of them was named Bjorn and the other Thorgrim. Illugi had Bjorn killed and Thorgrim's foot cut off. After that, Illugi rode home, and Onund sought no reprisals for this act. Hermund Illugason was very upset about his brother's death, and thought that, even though this had been done, Gunnlaug had not been properly avenged.

There was a man named Hrafn, who was a nephew of Onund of Mosfell's. He was an important merchant, and owned a ship which was moored in Hrutafjord.

That spring, Hermund Illugason rode out from home on his own. He went north over Holtavarda heath, across to Hrutafjord and then over to the merchants' ship at Bordeyri. The merchants were almost ready to leave. Skipper Hrafn was ashore, with several other people. Hermund rode up to him, drove his spear through him and then rode away. Hrafn's colleagues were all caught off-guard by Hermund. No compensation was forthcoming for this killing, and with it the feuding between Illugi the Black and Onund was at an end.

Some time later, Thorstein Egilsson married his daughter Helga to a man named Thorkel, the son of Hallkel. He lived out in Hraunsdal, and Helga went back home with him, although she did not really love him. She could never get Gunnlaug out of her mind, even though he was dead. Still, Thorkel was a decent man, rich and a good poet. They had a fair number of children. One of their sons was named Thorarin, another Thorstein, and they had more children besides.

Helga's greatest pleasure was to unfold the cloak which Gunnlaug had given her and stare at it for a long time. Now there was a time when Thorkel and Helga's household was afflicted with a terrible illness, and many people suffered a long time with it. Helga, too, became ill but did not take to her bed. One Saturday evening, Helga sat in the fire-room, resting her head in her husband Thorkel's lap. She sent for the cloak Gunnlaug's Gift, and when it arrived, she sat up and spread it out in front of her. She stared at it for a while. Then she fell back into her husband's arms, dead. Thorkel spoke this verse:

25. My Helga, good arm-serpent's staff,   *arm-serpent*: gold
    dead in my arms I did clasp.   bracelet; its *staff*:
    God carried off the life   woman
    of the linen-Lofn, my wife.   *linen-Lofn* (goddess):
    But for me, the river-flash's poor craver,   woman
    it is heavier to be yet living.   *river-flash*: gold; its
                                            craver: man

Helga was taken to the church, but Thorkel carried on living in Hraunsdal. As one might expect, he found Helga's death extremely hard to bear.

And this is the end of the saga.

Glossary

Althing – Iceland's general assembly; also called the
  'Thing'. At the annual Althing, the thirty-nine *godis*
  (local chieftains) reviewed and made new laws, and set
  fines and punishments.
beserk – a man who worked himself into an animal-like
  frenzy to increase his strength and make himself
  immune to blows from weapons.
drapa – a heroic poem in a complicated metre, usually
  composed in honour of kings, earls and other prominent
  people, or in memory of a loved one.
fetch – a personal spirit that often symbolized a person's
  fate or signalled impending doom. It could take various
  forms, sometimes appearing in the shape of an animal.
flokk – a short poem.
hersir – a local leader in western and northern Norway.
knorr – an ocean-going cargo vessel.
shieling – a hut in the highland grazing pastures away from
  the farm, where shepherds and cowherds lived in
  summer.
Winter Nights – the period of two days when winter began,
  around the middle of October. It was a particularly holy
  time of year, when sacrifices and social activities such as
  weddings took place.